Dec 18

For Jim, Grant, Alex,
and my little shark, Nate.
—TL

For our brother, Ryan. Thank you
for your fierce sense of humor.
—BC

 little bee books

An imprint of Bonnier Publishing USA
251 Park Avenue South, New York, NY 10010
Text copyright © 2018 by Becky Cattie and Tara Luebbe
Illustrations copyright © 2018 by Daniel Duncan
Manufactured in China   HH 1217
First Edition   10 9 8 7 6 5 4 3 2 1
Library of Congress Cataloging-in-Publication Data
Names: Cattie, Becky, author. | Luebbe, Tara, author. | Duncan, Daniel (Illustrator), illustrator.
Title: Shark Nate-O / by Becky Cattie and Tara Luebbe; illustrated by Daniel Duncan.
Description: First edition. | New York, NY: Little Bee Books, [2018]
Summary: Nate, who loves sharks, cannot swim, but with his brother's prodding, a good coach, and a lot of determination, he learns to swim like a shark.
Includes facts about sharks. | Subjects: | CYAC: Swimming—Fiction. | Sharks—Fiction. | Brothers—Fiction.
Identifiers: LCCN 2017003443 | Classification: LCC PZ7.1.C4638 Sh 2018 | DDC [E]—dc23 | LC record available at https://lccn.loc.gov/2017003443

ISBN 978-1-4998-0496-6
littlebeebooks.com
bonnierpublishingusa.com

SHARK NATE-O

by Tara Luebbe
and Becky Cattie

illustrated by
Daniel Duncan

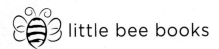

little bee books

Nate loved sharks.

He read shark books,

watched sharks on TV,

and at school.

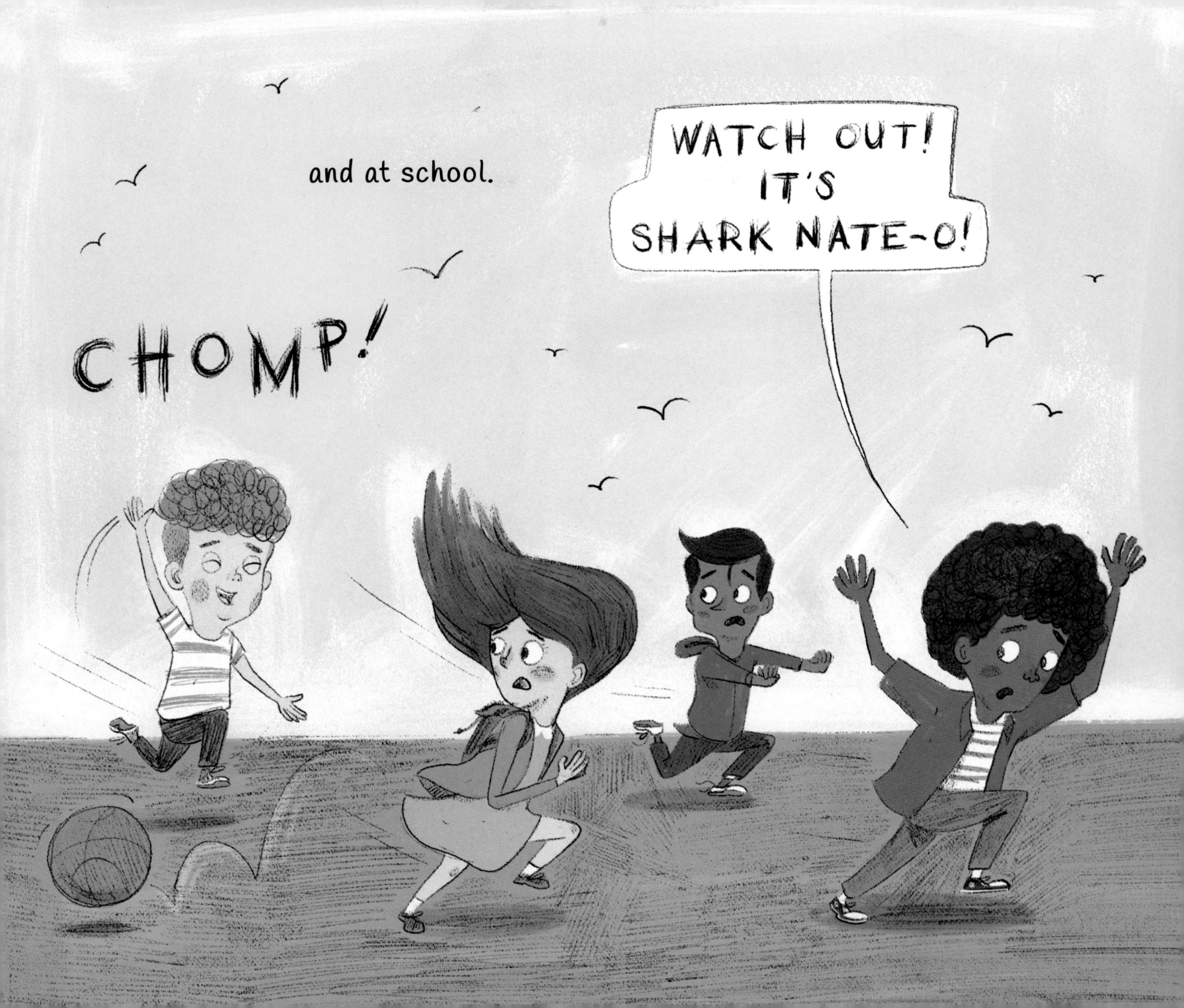

Chomp! Nate answered. But Alex was right. Luckily, Nate had a plan of attack.

On Monday at his first swim lesson, Nate told Coach Debra,
"I'm a shark. I was born swimming. Watch this."

He thrashed about like a thresher shark, but his fins failed, and his gills gurgled.

Nate wasn't frightful or bite-ful.
He didn't feel like a great white shark.
He felt like a great white wimp.

On Tuesday, Nate was nervous about getting back into the pool.

Sharks are fearless, he reminded himself, slowly testing the water.

Coach Debra showed him how to blow bubbles.
After a few mouthfuls of water, he got the hang of it.

Then Nate put his whole face in the water.

His eyes stung, but he adapted.

"All right," said Coach Debra.
"Now hold tight while I pull you."

On Wednesday, Nate kicked like a carnivore.

On Thursday, he floated fiercely.

On Friday, he paddled like a predator.

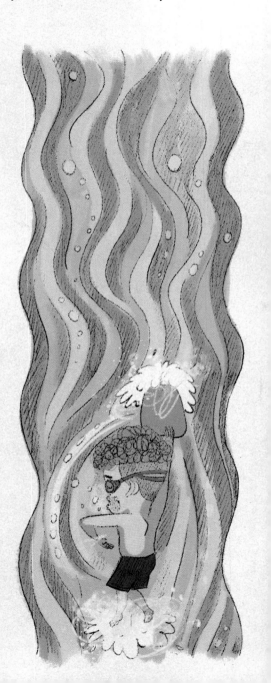

"Fin-tastic!" Coach Debra said.

Nate whispered
a tiny little CHOMP!

After practicing his tail off for weeks,
Nate decided he was ready to swim without any help.

Sharks must keep moving at all times or else . . .
Nate told himself, and he let go of the wall.

At first, he nosed around the shallow end like a big, slow Greenland shark.

But after a while, Nate began to find his stride.
He glided gracefully into deeper water like a blue shark.

Before long, he had it figured out. He even surprised himself when he ripped through the water like a speedy mako shark.

Nate could swim on his own!

But there was still
one problem....

"I need to swim with the Sharks."

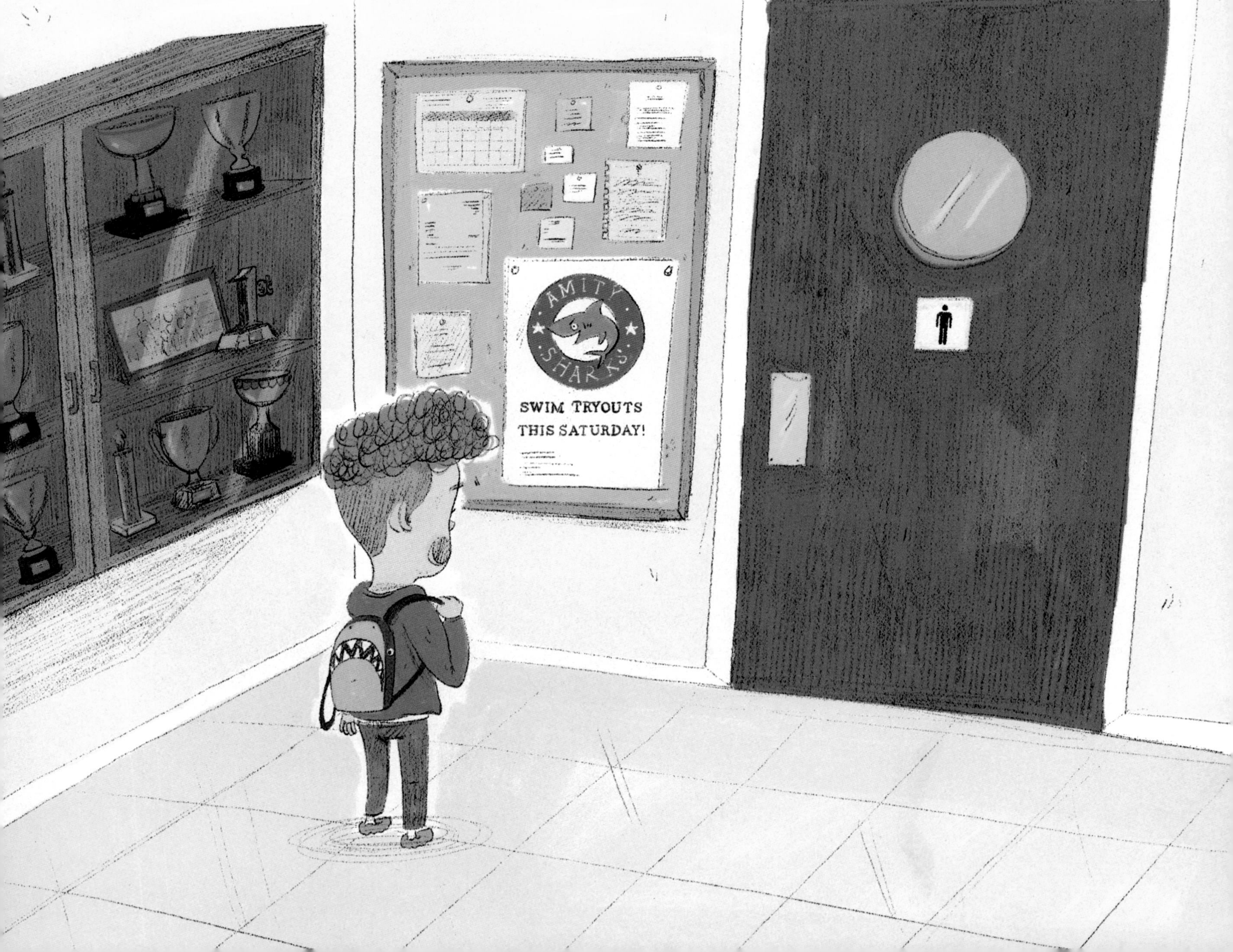

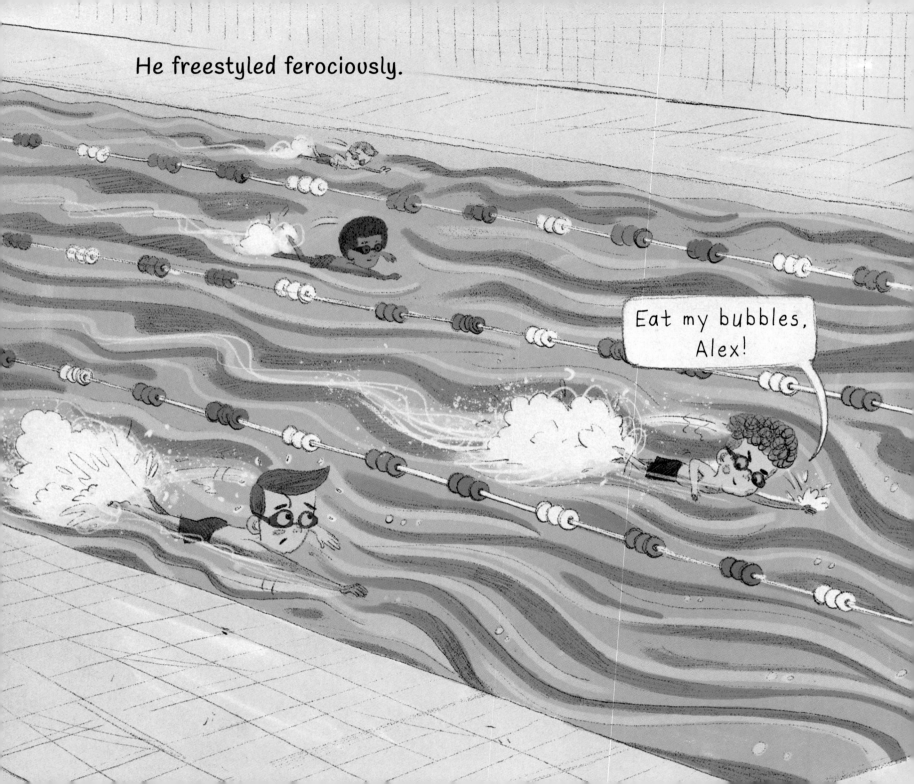

Nate smiled a big sharky grin. He had his bite back!

He didn't have to pretend anymore. . . .
He was Jawsome.

Nate's Shark Facts

Sharks have been living on Earth for 400 million years. They live in all of the world's oceans except the very coldest parts of the Antarctic. There are more than 500 different species of sharks, and scientists believe there are still more to be discovered.

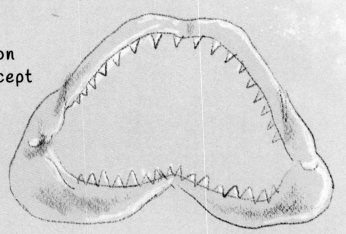

Thresher sharks hunt with their long tails. They whip and stun the fish so they can be easily eaten.

Greenland sharks are the longest-living species of sharks, with life spans between 272–512 years. They are among the slowest-swimming sharks, and their meat is toxic if eaten.

Sharpnose sevengill sharks have seven gill slits instead of five, and eyes that glow green in deep water.

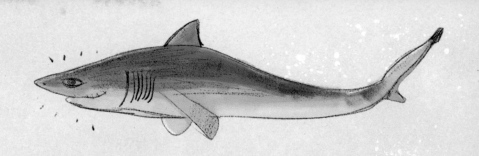

Shortfin mako sharks are the fastest swimmers. They can reach speeds up to 60 mph.

Blue sharks are the most graceful swimmers, but not the most graceful eaters. They often eat too much, vomit, and go back for more.

The cookiecutter shark has a circular jaw that attaches to prey and sucks out a perfect cookie-shaped hole of flesh from its victim.

The epaulette shark can use its fins to walk on land and is able to survive one hour without breathing.

Horn sharks' teeth turn purple from eating so many sea urchins.

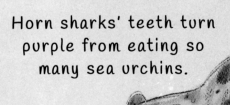

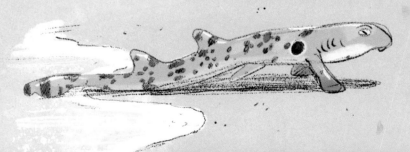